To my daughter, Alexa,
for when she fears the unknown.
—D.H.

This book is for my darling nephew, Chinua.
—D.B.G.

Published by Longmeadow Press, 201 High Ridge Road, Stamford, Connecticut 06904.

Book Design by Allison G. Russo

ISBN: 0-681-00755-9
Manufactured in Singapore
First Edition

0  9  8  7  6  5  4  3  2  1

# ARE YOU A MONSTER?

by Debra Hess
illustrated by D.B. Graves

Longmeadow Press

On the nights Molly's mother put her to bed,
she fluffed up the pillows beneath Molly's head.
She tucked in the covers, kissed Molly and said,

"I'll check in the closet for monsters."

On the nights Molly's father sent her to sleep,
he wished her sweet dreams and a sleep that was deep.
He pulled up her blankets and then he would creep . . .

under

the

bed . . .

to look for monsters.

Even on the nights Molly's brother was there
to snuggle her in with her rabbit and bear,
he'd turn off the light, and then he would stare,
out the window . . .

to check for monsters.

Molly asked about monsters, asked her mother and father, asked her brother "what are they and why do they bother to hide in the closet or under the bed or outside the window, and what are they fed?"

"Do they eat little girls in their beds in the night?
Will they gobble me whole or just take a bite?
Do they ever come out when the world is all light?
When I do meet a monster, should I smile or take flight?"

She asked:

"Are they huge?

Are they green?

Are they furry or hairy?

Are they slimy
and small?

Are they nasty
and scary?

Do they live
in the forest

or a crack
in a wall?"

But no one could tell her
about monsters at all.

NO
MONSTERS
ALLOWED
THIS MEANS
YOU!!

They just weren't sure.
They just didn't know
what a monster looked like
or if one would glow
in the dark of her room
on a wet rainy night,
when Molly was huddled
in wonder and fright.

They just knew that right before going to bed,
in order to sleep with no fear and no dread,
it was best to check everywhere
and then have it said . . .

that no monsters were lurking around.

One night, Molly woke to a fierce crack of lightning
and wind that was howling.
It was really quite frightening.
She took a deep breath, she smoothed back her hair,
she leapt from her bed with both rabbit and bear.
She went to the window where rain trickled in
and called to the storm through the deafening din.

**CRACK!**

"Are you a monster?" she asked.
And the rain answered back
as driplets and droplets
hit the house with a smack.

A lightning bolt struck and cracked open the sky,
and Molly leaned out of the window to cry:
"Are you a monster?" again.
But, her words went unheeded
so again Molly leaned out the window and pleaded.

"Are you a monster?

Please tell me—I really must know
if monsters live only in rain or in snow,
and what do they like and where do they go,
and what do they eat?  I really must know."

BOOM!

"I'll tell you," a voice from behind Molly said,
and she whirled and she turned to look at her bed.
A small furry creature about Molly's size,
with four furry arms, a mouth and two eyes . . .

was sitting
on Molly's bed.

"I hear you've been asking about us," it said.
Then it scratched at the fur on its quite furry head.
"I'm a monster, you know, and I'm here, as you see,
to answer the questions you have about me."

"You're a monster?" asked Molly. "You're not under the bed,
and you're not in a closet and I haven't fled
because I'm not frightened the way people said
I would be . . .

when I saw a monster."

"Ah, people," the monster said, and he sighed.
"The way that they talk, well, I've certainly cried.
When I hear how they plan and how they describe
how the moment they see a monster
they'll hide."

"It's really not fair, not fair at all.
You see, we're a mixed lot, some tall and some small.
Now some monsters are mean, but I've not ever seen,
a monster who eats little girls."

"That's a good thing to know," Molly said with a smile.
She sat next to the monster, they talked for awhile
about monster lives and about monster dreams,
and about how not everything is what it seems.

"Long ago," said the monster, "before we would sleep
we checked in the closets where people could creep,
we checked under beds, and in dresser drawers,
we checked all the cracks in the walls and the floors.

We looked everywhere
a person could be,
in the dark of the night,
because Molly, you see,
we were frightened of you,
of all people and places,
of anything new,
of any strange faces.

But one day we learned that some people are scary
and some are quite nice, even if they're not hairy.
I no longer look under beds before sleep.
I no longer think that a human would creep
into my home and into my bed.
Now, I think something different instead.
I think if the people who live above ground
would want to be friends with the monsters around . . .

life would be nicer."

"Much nicer," said Molly.
She yawned and she stretched,
and then she said, "golly".

It had been a long night. She had made a new friend.
She didn't see how she'd be able to send
him back to his home under the ground
it didn't seem fair now that she'd found
out the truth . . .

about monsters.

The monster and Molly lay down on the bed.
They each had a pillow for under their head.
Molly had rabbit and Monster had bear,
and between them they didn't have even one care.